A Job for Donald and Douglas

Learn to read with Thomas

EGMONT

We bring stories to life

First published in Great Britain 2008
by Egmont UK Limited
239 Kensington High Street, London W8 6SA
All rights reserved.

HiT entertainment

Thomas the Tank Engine & Friends™

CREATED BY BRITT ALLCROFT

Based on the Railway Series by the Reverend W Awdry
© 2008 Gullane (Thomas) LLC. A HIT Entertainment company.
Thomas the Tank Engine & Friends and Thomas & Friends are trademarks of Gullane (Thomas) Limited.
Thomas the Tank Engine & Friends and Design is Reg. U.S. Pat. & Tm. Off.

ISBN 978 1 4052 3789 5
1 3 5 7 9 10 8 6 4 2

Printed in Singapore

Learn to read with Thomas

This series of early learning story books draws on the 45 key words that children learn in the first year of the National Curriculum.

The stories contain repetition of these key words and phrases. This will help your child to recognise them, and to make the link between their sounds and their shapes on the page. Your child will also begin to predict what is coming next, thus connecting written and spoken words, enabling them to 'read'.

Listening to stories read aloud motivates children to want to read for themselves, and well-loved characters like Thomas encourage their interest in books.

To get the most out of the stories:

- read them with your child on several occasions;
- use a lively tone of voice and point to the words;
- encourage your child to read aloud the words he/she has learned.

Other activities to enjoy:

- **Follow the train tracks**
  Children can trace with a pencil from left to right in preparation for writing.
- **Find the pictures**
  Children can learn to observe small details in this activity.
- **Spot the difference**
  Children can compare two pictures, a skill used in reading when distinguishing the shapes of letters and words.

Donald and Douglas are twin engines.

One day, The Fat Controller comes to see them.

"I want one of you to go to the Yard," he says.

"I will go!" says Donald. "Please send me!"

"No, I will go," says Douglas. "Send me."

"I can go faster," says Donald. "Send me."

"No, I can go faster," says Douglas.

"Please send me!" say Donald and Douglas.

"Me! Me!" they say. "Send me!"

"Please be quiet!" says the Fat Controller.

"Who will I send?" he says to Thomas.

"I know who to send," says Thomas.

"Is it me? Is it me?" say Donald and Douglas.

"No, it is not you," says Thomas. "It is me!"

"I am fast. I am quick. Send me to the Yard!"

"I will!" says the Fat Controller. "Off you go, Thomas!"

These pictures look the same, but there are
5 differences in picture 2.

Can you spot them all?

Follow the train tracks with a pencil.
Start at the red flag.

Point to the things in the big picture.

Learn to read with Thomas

This pre-reading programme is designed to encourage an early confidence in reading. It features 40 of the frequent use-words as set out in the National Curriculum, plus key vocabulary from the Thomas Learning programme.

Read on with Thomas with the full range of titles:

Harold Shows Off
9781405237901

Really Useful Bertie
9781405237888

A Job for Donald and Douglas
9781405237895

Thomas and the Bees
9781405237871

Free Poster!

Reading with Thomas is as easy as ABC. To claim this attractive poster, log on to www.egmont.co.uk/learntoread. Offer ends 31st December 2008. Available while stocks last.

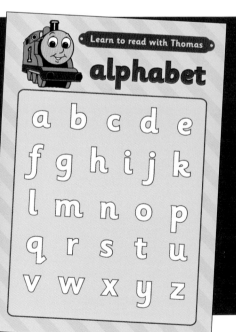

© 2008 Gullane (Thomas) Limited. A HIT Entertainment company.

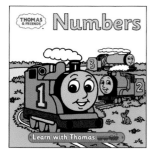

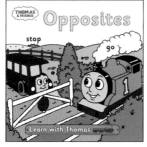
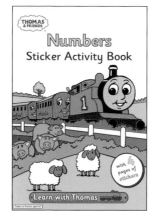
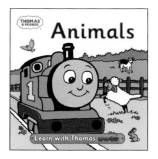